Jorge Harrington is an entrepreneur, father, and member of the Oglala Sioux Tribe, a Native American community. He is also an author, known for the self-published *Not for Kids Series* and *A Song of Scarlet*. Additionally, he owns Betaswitch.net, a platform where he assists recently divorced men in becoming the best versions of themselves. Currently, Jorge resides in Oregon with his son, teaching him how to recognize and seize opportunities.

I dedicate this book to my son, Braxton.

Jorge Harrington

A Room

A Collection of Horror Stories

AUSTIN MACAULEY PUBLISHERS™

LONDON • CAMBRIDGE • NEW YORK • SHARJAH

Ordering Information
Quantity sales: Special discounts are available on quantity purchases by corporations, associations, and others. For details, contact the publisher at the address below.

Publisher's Cataloging-in-Publication data
Harrington, Jorge
A Room

ISBN 9781649795861 (Paperback)
ISBN 9781649795878 (Hardback)
ISBN 9781649795885 (ePub e-book)

Library of Congress Control Number: 2023912912

www.austinmacauley.com/us

First Published 2023
Austin Macauley Publishers LLC
40 Wall Street
33rd Floor, Suite 3302
New York, NY 10005
USA

mail-usa@austinmacauley.com
+1 (646) 5125767

I want to acknowledge Daniel Frank, Gerald Whinery, Matt Mauney, Nick Harris, Ethan Hawke Branom, and Lacy Mauney. You all have given me advice that I will use for the rest of my life. You have made me laugh, and you have made me feel. Even though my passion is to write, you guys have never let me give up on my dreams.

Table of Contents

The Plant   11

The Purple Pill   25

The Emerald Child   58

He Rang   61

Shavings   73

Dragon Fever   91

No Trespassing   97

The Plant

There was a knock on Dirk's door. He didn't hear it because he had a telephone-headset over his ears and he was leaving a voicemail for a client. "Hello, my name is Dirk Looks-Twice and I'm reaching out to you because you recently showed interest in one of our products. If you will give me a call back at 801-872-4365, it would be much appreciated. Thank you for your time and help and have a nice day."

Dirk's door suddenly popped open and his roommate, Matt, poked his head in.

"I keep forgetting that you have a strange last name. Looks-Twice?"

"Take it up with my mother and my tribe," he said. "How can I help you?"

"Would you mind coming out here? I know you're working from home, but this affects all of us."

Before Dirk could respond, Matt disappeared and left his bedroom door ajar.

*****

The smell came from the kitchen. It was suffocating him. Dirk reached into his pocket and pulled out his inhaler.

He took a puff and it helped a little. The more he traveled deeper into the kitchen, the more his oxygen level was depleting. He had pulled his shirt over his mouth and nose.

"That's the smell of bleach," said Matt. He was leaning against the counter with arms crossed. Dirk noticed he didn't have anything covering his mouth. "My girlfriend is allergic to bleach. We need this gone, right away. How come you did this?"

"Where is she?"

"She's in my room with the door locked."

Dirk's eyes moved around in their socket, thinking of why it would smell like bleach. Finally, he knew why it did.

"Your garbage disposal wasn't working right. I thought it was clogged, so I poured Drano down it."

"So, it was Drano, not bleach."

"When I plugged it back in to turn on the switch, the disposal started smoking. I forgot to tell you about it. I thought the chemicals would eventually drain."

"Come here," Matt motioned with his hand and pointed at the layer of white and blue bubbles protruding out of the drain. "It's been like this for two days."

"We need a new garbage disposal," said Dirk.

"I don't want a garbage disposal; I want a new sink. Now would be the perfect time to go get one."

Dirk looked out the window and then at the clock. "I'll have to go now, otherwise it'll never get done."

"I guess those are the benefits of working from home during a pandemic."

"It was nice to work from home for a week, then it got old really quick."

"You can go get it and finish work later tonight."

Matt did make a great point. Dirk did not have much of a life to begin with, but since the pandemic, playing videogames was what everyone was doing. He thought if he had to play another hour of videogames, he was going to kill himself.

"Yeah, I will go, I have to get my inhaler refilled anyways, but if I lose my job. I'll throw you out of your own house and let you get the infection."

His roommate let out a laugh. "Sounds like a plan, dude. Thanks bro."

*****

Dirk pulled his sweater over his head. It read:

I SURVIVED THE 2020 EARTHQUAKE

He chose this sweater, so he could get people's mind off the pandemic by giving them a comic relief. The situation the world was in was making everyone act crazy and desperate.

"Don't forget your mask!" screamed Matt from the bedroom.

Dirk Looks-Twice's keys were hanging on a tiny hook next to the front door. Next to the keys, was where his mask hung. It would be his first time wearing it.

It was mandatory.

The streets were bare. People were quarantined in their homes, at the grocery store, or dead. It made Dirk sick to his stomach. His girlfriend was right for leaving him. He did not have a lot of money for himself, especially during a pandemic, what made him think his ex-girlfriend was going to benefit from the relationship?

"I'll be right back! I got you!"

*****

There were two lines. These lines weren't as long as the lines in the early morning. That's if Dirk listened to what they said on the news. He stood twelve people from the door. At the front of the door were people dressed in gowns, gloves, and goggles.

With a thermometer, they scanned everyone's forehead for fever. Then they would ask them a series of questions. Last, they would poke their finger with a needle and test their body for any antibodies, if they didn't have a fever.

Dirk looked up at the sign of the grocery store. There were signs above the logo, it read:

GIVE BLOOD!
SAVE LIVES!
YOU COULD BE THE CURE!

"I think I already had the virus back in the day," said a man in the line. Dirk only stared straight ahead and listened to the people in masks talk. "I thought it was the flu at first, but I had blood in my mucus, and I had fever for days."

A woman began to speak after the man. She must have overheard him and felt it to express her opinion. "He better shut his mouth, otherwise he's going to start a panic. I can't afford to get it. I already lost my job."

The line moved forward a few people.

"Ouch! That hurt!" screamed the customer at the front of the line. "You can't treat us like this! We're people, not cattle!"

"Mam, everyone who isn't infected will be poked the same way you did."

The customer let out a frustrated breath and stormed her way into the store. Her mask was protruding in and out as she wiped down the handle of her shopping cart.

"Keep moving forward!" yelled the experts at the entrance.

"If there was ever a chance to get into a relationship, it's gone now," said a girl. "How are the guys supposed to see me with my mask on?"

"Don't take off your mask or you'll break the law," said her mother.

"I heard they arrested a man because his mask accidentally fell off," said the man behind them.

"Fake news!" yelled a stranger a few people down from them.

All these comments were making Dirk wish it was all over. This all will go away one way or the other.

"Next!" said the expert, letting people leave the store after they forced her to wash their hands for the hundredth time.

*****

It was a process that made people crazy. *This pandemic is going to change human culture for sure,* thought Dirk.

He washed his hands, got his temperature taken, and they poked his finger and took some of his blood. There was no sign of the virus in his blood sample. Which means he is not the cure that can save people. This thought made him laugh on his way to the pharmacy.

Dirk wished there were a cure for asthma. He was considered high risk during this pandemic.

Surprisingly, there was not a giant line at the pharmacy window. However, there was a sneeze-guard that was in front of the window. Double protection.

Refilling his inhaler took no longer than five minutes. He pushed the box into his back pocket and pulled the old inhaler out of his front pocket. There were zero puffs left in it.

There was a trash bin a few aisles away. Standing next to the trashcan, was a girl.

Not just any girl, but a gorgeous girl. There were tattoos all over her body. It was not the tattoos on her neck or the beauty of her eyes that made Dirk stare at her. It was the absence of a mask that made him stare.

Her smile and the twirling of her hair made Dirk know that she wanted him to come over and talk to her.

He did.

*****

The girl disappeared into the aisle next to the trashcan, but something made Dirk feel as if she was waiting for him to follow her. He threw the inhaler into the trash and popped his head around the corner. "Hello?"

There was no reply from her. She only gestured him over with her finger. Nobody was around. She was going to cause a panic in the store is they saw her without a mask.

"Where's your mask?" asked Dirk.

She gave another smile but did not answer back. Instead, she grabbed Dirks hand, the one with the Band-Aid on it, and tore it off. Dirk did not have time pull his hand away before she stuck his finger in her mouth.

*****

"What are you doing?" asked Dirk. He could feel her strength when she tightened her grip around his wrist. It felt like she could rip his arm right off if he pulled his arm from her. "Let go!"

With her left hand she grabbed Dirk around the neck and held him still. He could not breathe. He grabbed her wrist and struggled. She lifted him into the air and spit out his finger.

The girl smiled, but this time. She showed her teeth. A pair of fangs protruded, making her look like a snake. Her eyes turned purple and red. The white fangs plunged themselves into his neck. Dirk cried out, but it sounded like a broken bell.

*****

There was a ten-year-old girl named Susie walking down an aisle. In front of her was a trashcan. The same trashcan that Dirk tossed his empty inhaler in. She wore a mask with strawberries on it.

It was crackers she wanted. The clerk told her and her mother where to find them. They also needed to find toilet paper. Crackers were on aisle 10 and toilet paper was on aisle 1. They split up, so they could get at least one package of toilet paper, before they were all gone.

When Susie turned the corner of aisle 10, she saw a girl biting a boy on the neck. She could see the girl's neck muscles working up and down as she drank. Her eyes stared straight at Susie, but she was not 'looking' at her. The eyes looked intoxicated. A shot of potent dopamine was running through her brain.

Suddenly, the girl pulled the boy from her mouth and dropped him to the floor. Susie was frozen with fear. She watched as the girl motioned with her finger to be quiet, or she will get her too. The girl took the same finger she had to her lips and ran it across her neck.

Susie almost screamed. Instead, she passed out after watching the girl's eyes and teeth return to normal.

*****

"Damn kid! She almost blew it for me, I have not had a drink in so long. It is too risky to finish him off now that I have been seen. I guess he'll have to become like me and go through what I go through."

Her voice was so loud in Dirk's head. It sounded like there were two people talking at one time. Her voice and a dark deep voice. The sound of her moving away from his body, was giving him a headache.

Suddenly, all the hurt went away, and Dirks eyes popped open. He took a deep breath and his nerves calmed. When he stood up, it felt like he was floating upward. The girl was gone, but there was a different girl laying on the floor.

He noticed she did not have a mask on her face. Dirk also noticed that he was in an aisle of mirrors. His hand went to the side of his neck and felt two sticky holes. There was no way he could see how bad the damage was because his reflection was completely gone.

Suddenly, he could hear the voice inside of the unconscious girl's head. It was all a scream. Dirk put his hands over his ears as he ran out of the aisle. Only it felt like he teleported.

The scream died down and was fading. However, a barrage of other voices entered his mind. The voices were the thoughts of the customers inside of the store.

"I hope our president gets the virus."

"My boyfriend is going to be so surprised when I tell him I'm pregnant. He'll finally stop playing video games."

"I'm so smart. I bought all my supplies months before."

"This is not what I wanted. I want a zombie apocalypse."

"Figure it out!"

"What are you looking at?"

Dirk turned his head away after he made eye contact with a customer. He spotted the door that was under the EXIT sign.

How was he going to get out of the store without being seen by others? The door was five aisles away. As soon as Dirk took a step toward the door. Not more than three seconds went by before he had a grip on the handle.

He pulled the door open and walked out into the night.

*****

"Did you tell him about the sink?" asked Matt's girlfriend.

Matt looked up from his phone and rolled his eyes. "Of course I did. He's out getting a new one."

"I bet he'll get the wrong one," she continued.

"Just wait and see."

"Just wait and see? Wait for what? For you to be a man and get him out of the house already?"

"We already talked about this; we need him to pay the rent. Where do you think most of the money is coming from?"

"Yeah, you told me about that. But what if I want to have a baby?"

Matt only took a breath and remained silent.

"That's what I thought you'd do. We're having a baby and he's getting out of here."

"What am I supposed to do? We're in the middle of a pandemic."

"If you love me, you'd tell him to get out. Do you love me?"

"You know I do."

"It doesn't feel like it. He doesn't even have a girlfriend; don't you find that a little creepy?"

She was really pushing it. Matt got up from the bed and went into the bathroom. As soon as he closed the door, his girlfriend was already knocking on the door and demanding to be let in.

"Give me a minute," he protested.

"Why did you walk away from me when I said that?"

There was no answer, just the sound of Matt's stream, hitting the toilet water.

"You're disgusting! Do you know what I really feel? I feel you two are trying to suffocate me with all the bleach."

Matt's girlfriend was startled by the sound of the bathroom door as it flung open. "That doesn't make any sense."

"You didn't wash your hands."

There was a smile on her face as she watched Matt give her a nasty look and then turn on the water.

"Will you kick him out?" she continued. "Kick him out and I'll give you a big surprise."

DING! DONG!

*****

"Who could that be?" asked Matt's girlfriend. "Is it your parents?"

"I don't think so," answered Matt. There was fear in his voice.

He stared down the hallway from his room. Matt's girlfriend poked her head out too.

"Aren't you going to answer it?"

"Could it be your dad?"

"What if it's Dirk? I'm scared."

Matt shoved her back into the room and shut the door on her. He approached the front door and hesitated to put his hand on the doorknob.

When he looked over his shoulder, he saw his girlfriend pointing at him. It was her way of telling him to hurry up and answer the door.

He did.

*****

"Dirk, bro. You scared me," said Matt. He looked over his shoulder again and this time, his girlfriend shut herself in the room.

"How did I scare you?"

Matt thought his voice sounded inviting and hypnotic. "Dude, you live here. You don't need to ring the doorbell."

There was no response from Dirk. He looked Matt dead in the eye, which was making him feel uncomfortable. "Did you get the sink?"

"I sure did. Let's talk about it inside."

"Is that blood on your shirt?"

"Let me in and we'll talk about everything."

"Why is he acting like this? He looks pale. I swear he's smiling under that facemask."

"I guess you better come in then," said Matt, jokingly. He moved aside and let Dirk walk by him.

*****

The smell of Drano filled up Dirk's and Matt's lungs. Only this time, it did not choke him. He did not need air in his lungs to breathe anymore.

Dirk reached into his pocket and pulled out the new inhaler. He crushed it in his hand with ease. It made a mild 'POP' sound and then he discarded it into the trashcan.

"Is the sink in the car?" asked Matt, who entered the kitchen. "Did you run to the kitchen? I could have sworn we were just outside talking."

"Why did you say those things about me?" asked Dirk. He looked over his shoulder at Matt.

Matt blinked and when he opened his eyes, Dirk was in his face.

"What are you talking about?" coughed Matt.

"Let me tell you one thing before you go," said Dirk. He grabbed Matt by the neck and arm and held him tight. His face transformed. Fangs protruded out of his mask, revealing his face, completely. His eyes turn to crimson. "I'm not just some plant you have laying around the house, I'm essential."

Matt's body squirmed in his grasp. Like a rat does, after the life has been squeezed out of it from a python. He tried to scream, but nothing came out. Dirk only shushed him.

"I know you're scared, but don't worry. I got you."

The fangs pierced his roommates' neck.

*****

Matt's girlfriend stood at the door with her ear against the wood. She desperately tried to zero in on their conversation from the comfort of the bedroom. Her hands were cupped around her ear.

"He forgot to bring the sink," said Matt, through the door.

She moved her head away from the door, concerned, "Did you tell him?"

"Did I tell him that he no longer lives here? You better believe it."

"Quit playing, babe."

"I don't play. Now we can have a baby. Open the door and let us make one."

Her eyes rolled at his comment. *"Boys are such perverts. That's all they want is sex!"* She opened the door and screamed at the red eyes and teeth.

*****

RING! RING! RING!

Dirk opened his bedroom door. The light on his headset was blinking red and ringing. He sat down at the edge of his bed, in front of his work computer. Matt's girlfriend's neck was still attached to his fangs.

He took one last gulp and spit out the shriveled body. It sounded like old leaves crumbling as she hit the ground, under his desk.

The phone was answered on the fourth ring, "Thank you for calling, Betaswitch.net, my name is Dirk Looks-Twice… yes that's my real name… I am doing good, thanks for asking… yeah, it was me who called you earlier. I appreciate you giving me a call back."

The Purple Pill

Todd stared out of his bedroom window and into the window of his neighbor. He could see a wooden desk with cords braided downward and into the nearest outlet. The light from two screens revealed a man's face, who rapidly typed on a keyboard.

"How come you keep acting like that?" asked Caroline. She awkwardly entered in the room.

"Act like what, exactly?" asked Todd. He turned his attention to his wife and raised an eyebrow.

"Never mind," she said, annoyed, walking into her closet.

"I'm acting weird?" asked Todd, pointing out the window. "That guy over there is the weird one. He has a high paying job, a giant house, and low-key public fame. Still, he does not have a wife. I think he is a serial killer. Did you see all the cats he has crawling around his house? He gets it one way or the other, if you know what I am saying."

There was a sigh from the closet, instead of the normal dialogue that happens when Todd spoke of the neighbor. There was no, "be nice Todd. He's successful and that's attractive," speech. There was no response to his comment.

It had been six years, and this was the first time he did not hear retaliation from Caroline.

He turned away from the window and was about to go into the closet after her, but she emerged with the luggage she got for Christmas last year.

"What's all this?" Todd was taken aback; he already knew the answer.

Caroline appeared as though she were about to cry, but she took a deep breath and all the emotions left her. "I'm going to try and sound like I'm not a heartless bitch, but I think we need to talk."

*****

"Talk about what?" Todd's stomach felt like it was flipping within him.

"If you'll sit down and listen to me, I'll explain everything."

"Explain what?" he gulped. His knees weakened and before he knew it, he felt his backside it the bed.

Caroline opened the suitcase and then grabbed a handful of clothes as she spoke. "I don't think I can do this anymore. I know it may feel like I'm being heartless, but I've felt this way for two years."

"What way?" he asked. His face in his hands.

"Numb? Is that a way of putting it?"

"Wait a minute," Todd put his hands up and got down on his knees. "You don't love me anymore?"

"Please do not cry, Todd. God-dammit. You're such a pussy!" screamed Caroline. She threw arms full of clothes into the suitcase, almost emptying out the dresser completely.

Todd thought she was crying, but she was laughing. He didn't say anything. Instead, he cried into his hand. "You want a divorce?"

She shrugged and put a finger in her mouth. Something, she did when she was nervous or withholding information.

"What if we went to counseling?"

"I don't think it's going to do any good, to be honest."

"Why?"

"I don't know how to explain it."

"What about the kids?"

"What about them? None of them are yours."

It was that comment that caused Todd to beg. "Please don't do this to me! I am sorry! I am so sorry! I'll do anything! Please don't take them away from me!"

"They're not your kids, Todd."

"Don't say that! Don't say that! They're my kids, I raised them since they were babies."

"They're almost all teenagers," she said, zipping up the suitcase. "They can barely remember to do their chores, what makes you think they'll remember all those years."

Words could not describe the state of mind Todd was in. His hands were shacking.

"I beg you! Please don't *leave* me! I love you! I love you with all my heart! Oh God!"

"I'm not leaving you, Todd."

His face pulled away from his hands. He wiped them on his shorts and raised his eyebrow to Caroline. "Then why are you packing up the suitcases?"

"I packed all of your clothes. You're leaving."

*****

"This is my house," said Todd. He was in shock. "You can't kick me out of my own house."

"I'm not kicking you out of the house," said Caroline. She placed the suitcases in front of Todd and crossed her arms. Waiting patiently.

"What do you mean?"

She did not respond. Todd stood up and got closer to Caroline.

"What do you mean?"

She did not respond. Todd reached up and grabbed her arm and pulled her toward him. "Ouch!"

Suddenly, the bedroom door burst open and two police officers emerged.

"Let her go!" said the police officer. He had his hand on the top of his taser. The other police officer has his hand on his gun.

"I'm not hurting anyone. Did you call the cops on me?"

Caroline did not respond.

The two police officers grabbed Todd by the arms and handcuffed him.

"Am I under arrest? I didn't do anything! Why are you doing this? Ouch!"

Todd was pushed to his knees. One officer had his arm twisted while they were securing the cuffs around his wrists. He looked up and saw his neighbor was looking up from his computer screen. He must have watched the entire thing.

"Hey! I did not do anything! Help me!"

All three kids walked into the room. The oldest had her cell phone pressed against her chest. Todd knew it was her who called the cops.

The police officers ripped Todd up from the ground, dislocating his right shoulder. They dragged him from the room and then from the house. All Todd could think about was the smile on Caroline's face.

That smile was filled with evil.

*****

"Did you see on Facebook that Todd was abusing his wife?" asked Mildred. She rolled her chair into her coworkers' cubicle.

"No way? Really?" answered Sherry. Her cubicle seemed to feel more like a breakroom, than a work area. "Show me on your phone so I don't get into trouble."

"Read it and weep," said Mildred, handing over her phone.

It read:

I just want all of you to know that Todd Baitmen is an abuser. He grabbed me in a way that made me feel uncomfortable. I know it has been a few weeks since I came out about it, but I feared what people would think of me. I never thought I would be in this position. I hear on the news about spousal abuse and how it can affect you and worse, how it can affect your children. They are not even his kids and I believe he would have hurt them too if my daughter had not called the police. She is so brave. She is my little warrior. She is a fighter just like her mother. Please stand

Sherry looked up from the phone. Mildred swore she saw her coworkers jaw hit the floor and her eyes pop out. "He did that?"

"That's what she said happened," answered Mildred. "I believe her. I knew Todd was a pervert."

"What if he tries to abuse one of us?"

"He isn't going to abuse anybody anymore. I guarantee it."

"How would you know that?" Sherry raised an eyebrow.

"We have to warn everyone. I'm going to email this to HR and our manager."

"I'm scared," Sherry started typing at an unsettling pace. "What if we get into trouble?"

"Stop getting booty-tickled. Nobody will know it came from us."

"How are you going to do that?"

"Just watch the master," said Mildred. She got up and walked over to a cubicle, across the aisle and down another row of cubicles.

"Hey Bryan, how are you?" She asked leaning on the side of the desk.

Bryan didn't move his body, but Mildred could see that his eyes shifted to her, giving her his full attention. "Can I help you?"

"I was wondering if you were having trouble with your email."

He shifted his gaze back to the computer screen and clicked on his email icon. "I don't see anything wrong. I'm not having trouble."

Mildred laughed, "You're so funny. Hey, listen, Will you let me hop on?"

Bryan gulped. *She may have a gorgeous body, but she has a terrible first name,* he thought. "Uh… um… hop on what exactly?"

"You know… it… on your computer… so I can send an email to myself to see if it will work."

"… Oh… yeah… of course," said Bryan, standing up from his seat.

"I love you forever, Bryan," she said, giving Bryan a seductive smirk.

*****

"What did you do?" asked Sherry. Her eyes were darting in every direction. Hoping she would not be spotted by Todd.

"I sent a snapshot to HR and our boss," answered Mildred. "What if he abuses us? I hate the way he looks around the room. Sometimes I feel he is looking at me. I wanted him gone from the beginning."

"It did creep me out when he would talk to me in the morning. I just want him to leave me alone."

"We'll find out if it works at two today."

"Is that what time he comes in?"

"I don't know, you're the one who sits across from him." Mildred pushed herself back into her cubicle.

*****

Todd walked to his cubicle. His eyes were glazed over and puffy from sobbing. His shoulder hurt from being dislocated. Whenever he would lift his arm up a sharp twinge of pain would shoot through him. There were times he didn't want to turn his head.

"Good morning, Sherry," said Todd out of habit.

"Thanks," responded Sherry. It took all of her might not to scream for help.

The computer booted up and so did all the work icons. His email gave a 'ping' notifying him that he had an urgent message. Todd thought he was ready for anything. Being thrown out of your home by your wife. Caroline did it with no trace of regret. What could be worse than that?

Not only was the email urgent, but it was from his manager. It read:

Todd,

Don't bother clocking in. As soon as you get this message, please come straight to my office first.

Head Supervisor

*****

"You wanted to see me?" asked Todd. Even though he could see the Head Supervisor through the office window, he knocked and opened the door a crack. It was big enough to only fit his mouth in.

"Please come in and have a seat," she said typing madly on the keyboard.

Todd felt like he was going to up-chuck his meal he had the night before.

He sat down in a tiny chair that was in front of his boss' enormous desk. Was it enormous? Or was it an illusion, brought on by the unfortunate recent events?

"I wanted to talk to you before HR talks to you," she said. Her arms were crossed, protecting her core, when she came and stood in front of her desk. In front of Todd. "A little bird told me that you were abusing your wife."

This time, Todd gagged. It was not enough to make anything come up, but it was enough for his boss to go retreating behind her desk. "A little bird?"

"A little bird, that's what I said. It told me everything, I need to know. You are a threat to everyone in this building and should be ashamed of yourself. I have no choice but to release you of your contract with the company."

"Don't do this to me, please! I beg you! I don't know what I did to deserve this."

"You sound just like my ex-husband," she said. Her finger was pointing at him like it was a firearm. "You have fifteen minutes to go and pick up your things from your desk. Security will escort you from the building after that time is up."

"God, please! Please don't do this to me!"

"On your way back to your desk, will you let Bryan know, I want to speak to him next."

*****

Todd walked out of the courthouse with tears in his eyes. There were protesters outside of the capital building across the way. More than a thousand people were yelling, screaming, and waving signs above their heads.

It was hard to see where he parked with all the bodies in the parking lot. The people filled the streets. A crew from a YouTube channel were asking the protestors for the reason they felt the need to come out and protest during a pandemic.

"We're being oppressed! We are being silenced! Wake up America!" shouted a protester.

"Why do you feel like you need to protest? You aren't practicing social distancing very well," the YouTuber put his mic in front of the protester.

"Leave me alone! Leave all of us alone! Wake up America!"

"It's been sixty days since I had my last paycheck! Unlock my job!"

The YouTuber put his mic in front of four people's mouths, but they ignored him, and his questions and continued to rant and rave. "The cure for Corona Virus, is to drink a Modelo!"

Todd pushed past some people so he could get by. There were a bunch of girls singing in a circle and would swing their arms backwards and shake their wrists about their heads. He gently tapped one of the girls on the shoulder and said, "Excuse me. I'm just trying to get through."

"You touched me! Mom! This man groped me!"

The girl's mother stopped screaming at the top of her lungs and looked Todd dead in the eye. "He did what?"

"I don't know what you're talking about," said Todd. "I'm just trying to get home."

"You're a pervert!"

"I just lost my kids today! Have you no heart?"

"I'm glad your kids got taken away. A good man is a dead man. May God have mercy on your soul!"

"Hold up a minute!" interrupted the YouTuber. He came over with his mic and shoved it in front of Todd's mouth. "You lost your kids?"

Todd looked at the crew of teenagers and then at the teen with a mic in his hand. The logo of the channel read on his shirt, ONE-SHOE-MAN. Instantly, Todd looked down at the kid's feet to see if he had only one shoe on. He found out that the YouTube lived up to his name.

He nodded.

"Did they die? Are you coming out to protest too? How come you are here? Where are you going?"

"They didn't die," Todd wailed. "I lost them in court today."

"Wait a minute, you're telling me that you lost your kids today in court?"

"Technically they're not mine, but I love them like they were my own."

"What happened?"

He began to cry. "I did everything right! I don't know what I did to deserve this. I can't see them, but I have to pay for them?"

Suddenly, a protestor swung her purse and struck Todd in the side of the head. Another protestor screamed at the top of her lungs. "You're pussy!"

"Look at me!" said One-Shoe-Man. "There is a guy you need to talk to about all of this."

"I've talked to everyone. Every lawyer, everyone, I… I'm done. I can't."

"This guy isn't a lawyer. Here's his card." One-Shoe-Man pulled a red card from his pocket. "But he's been around the block if you know, what I mean."

"I don't know what you mean," said Todd, taking the card from the lad.

It had a question on one side, and the name on the other side.

The front side read: AGAIN?

On the back side, it read: PROFESSOR TINMAN.

*****

Todd figured the protesting would only last another hour, so he grabbed some tacos from a nearby taco truck and waited. His food was gone within five minutes. Now it was hours later, and more people began showing up with signs and flags. The sun was beginning to set, but the protesters were not showing any signs of slowing down.

He pulled out the card he was given earlier. If he still had a plate of tacos in his hand, he would have dropped them. The card showed an arrow, instead of the name. It acted like a compass.

Through the crowd, Todd walked. Looking up from the card and following the path it was leading him down. It pointed down a dark alley and it was out of sight from the public eye. Todd thought he would not have found this place if it had not been for the mysterious arrow.

At the end of the alley way, was a black tent. A wooden sign was propped up next to the entrance with the same question painted across the front of it like the card, AGAIN?

The arrow was blinking and within a few second, then it faded away and the name reappeared, PROFESSOR TINMAN.

Suddenly, the tent flap blew open and somebody Todd recognized emerged from the black hole in the tent. It was his neighbor. The one who always peeked over his computer screen and into their home. The neighbor looked at him had a something in his hand. At first, he didn't notice Todd standing there and almost revealed what he held. When he did, he quickly tightened his grasp on it and shoved it into his pocket. Todd was only able to give him an awkward look before the neighbor disappeared into the crowd of protestors.

What reason would he have to be here? Todd asked himself. *What reason do I have to be here? What was he trying to hide in his pocket?*

"Come forward," said a voice from within the tent.

*****

What do I have to lose? Todd asked himself as he hesitated to enter. Everything in his body was telling him to enter, which scared him more than ever.

Go in, you shithead. You lost your job, you lost your house, and you lost your kids. What else can go wrong? Why can't I move?

"Don't fear me boy," said the voice. "Your fear has already come to pass. Come forward."

It was like he was being pulled with an imaginary lasso. Todd felt like he was falling into a black abyss. Suddenly, he stopped moving. In front of him appeared a table and chairs. They were made of blackwood and were dimly lit by a candle.

Todd looked at the flame and instantly felt queasy. He bent over the table and heaved. Each one felt like an uppercut to chest and neck. They were not all dry heaves.

When it was all over. There was something laying on the table and covered in taco-bile. It was a glowing blue pill.

"Have a seat," said the voice.

His body went limp and the chair folded into a bed. Leather straps protruded out and bound his legs, chest, and wrists. Up on a stage. He could see the silhouette of a man in a top hat and a skeleton suit standing in a spotlight. He had a black and white cane in his hand and was pointing it at Todd.

"Let me out of here!" screamed Todd.

With a swish of his cane, a gag appeared in Todd's mouth and silenced him almost immediately.

"Todd Baitmen! The time for talk is over!" said the man in the skeleton suit. "I've come to give you the pill that will open your eyes. I am Professor Tinman, and I will set your mind free!"

*****

"And then… Todd… came and told me to go to the office… and uh… um… and they; she like… I got fired," said Bryan. He could barely hold his head up.

The protestors were screaming, accusing each other of misconduct, and waving signs around outside, while Bryan motioned to the bartender to refill his beer glass. He was enjoying the peace and quiet. Every so often, Bryan would look out the window and wonder what exactly the people are protesting.

"That's too bad," said the bartender. "I'm sure you'll figure it out. Do you want me to keep them coming?"

"My wife left me."

The bartender only gave a deep breath and listened to the poor souls' troubles.

"It was a few months back," continued Bryan. "My coworker, Todd, was… um… let go for abusing his wife. They had to call the cops on him and everything. I don't really care much for the guy. If he abused her, then he should be punished to the full extent of the law. Hiccup!"

Bryan took a deep breath, drank his entire glass of beer, swallowed two times, and then let out all the air from his nose. The hiccups seem to disappear.

The bartender poured another glass and waited for more story to come out of Bryan's mouth. He listened to this poor man, because it was better than staring at the eye sore outside the window.

"I came home and told her what happened," continued Bryan. "She acted like she was torn up about it. A part of me believed her. It wasn't until a few weeks, that I found out that she had been having an affair for two years of our… um… marriage."

"We have a state where adultery is illegal, and I thought I was going to get justice. Except when she cried to the judge, that law did not apply to her. Instead, they garnished my wages, took my kids away from me, I have to pay her alimony and child support, and I was kicked out of my own house that I bought years before I even met the bitch."

The bartender watched as Bryan bowed his head and stared at the empty glasses beneath himself. He picked one up and poured it full. Bryan looked surprised when he refilled his cup too.

"On the house," he said. "In fact, this whole bottle and one of your choice is on the house. You are the first one I have met that is finally speaking my language. I still pay for alimony; even after she found a guy willing to pay for all her expenses. He buys everything for my daughter and my money that the government is twisting my arm to pay, just gets put into her pocket. There is nothing I can do. Not to mention all the shame, I got after we divorced. My reputation was ruined by a post on social media."

The bartender threw is glass back and poured himself another drink.

"I'm sorry to hear that," said Bryan. He looked the bartender in the eyes and saw that they were the same sad eyes he had been staring at in the mirror. "My reputation hasn't been ruined."

Both men clinked glasses together.

"It hasn't happened yet."

"Um… let's just hope for the best."

A bell rang above the door. All the shouting and chants could be heard as the doors swung open. It cut through the bar with a razor-sharp knife without remorse. Bryan and the bartender looked to see who entered.

A young lady stepped in. She paused and looked at both men, seductively. Her body was covered in black tattoos, except for her face. Both men could not help but look and admire the curves of her ample chest and backside. If they paid close attention to her face, they would have seen that it was painted pale white and her lips and eyes were stained black. The bartender was reminded of his daughter and quickly looked away, so he would not think impure thoughts about her.

"Hey, cutie," she said, smiling. "How about a drink?"

*****

Professor Tinman sat at the vomit covered table. He pointed at the blue pill that was in front of Todd. The blue pill was the size of a silver half dollar. It glowed bright with a neon blue color.

"This is your problem my good sir. You have been conditioned to accept and swallow the blue pill. Anytime you feel a trauma in your soul, commonly brought on by heartbreak or a death in the family, the blue pill will reveal itself, like it has now."

Todd's eyes shot toward the blue pill. He could not believe that thing came out of his body. He then looked at the man in the skeleton suit and was reminded of a cartoon movie he watched when he was a child. The movie was called *The Witchdoctor*.

"I bet you're probably thinking I'm some sort of Witchdoctor. Far from it, Todd. When you take the pill like I have, your life will change forever. You will transform into what the world perceives you as. The world looks at me as a circus freak and needs to die as soon as possible. They speak shaming language that strips the flesh from my bones!"

The skeleton man undid his white tie and unbuttoned his shirt black shirt. "I was red, born in a world painted black and white. These are my bones! Why do they see me this way?"

"Um… ga…" Todd mumbled. He saw the ribcage that was under the shirt. A black infected hole was oozing out blood into nothingness, where his heart should have been.

"What did you say? Oh, you cannot speak because I have gagged you. Let me get that," said Professor Tinman. He waved his hand and the gag disappeared.

Todd gasped for air as the mechanism transformed back into a chair.

"Sorry, that had to happen," said Professor Tinman. He buttoned up his shirt and sat in front of Todd. "There are four ways a man can think in this world. The most common is the blue pill. Ninety-seven percent of world have lived their entire lives on it."

"You get to stay in fantasy land. No accountability for your actions and always blaming others. You *feel* more than you *think*."

Todd looked all around to see if he could run away, but there was no exit. He looked at Professor Tinman and then spoke, "What are the other colors? What pill did you take?"

"I am the color red and it's the pill that I highly recommend."

Bryan hiccupped as he watched the young lady, sit right next to him. He didn't know if it was the way the bartender reacted when he stared at her for more than three seconds, he didn't know if it was of her age, and he didn't know if it was because she was gorgeous, despite the tattoos and face paint. Bryan knew that he didn't feel comfortable with her presence.

"Let's party," she said. She smiled seductively. "I'm old enough, that I can assure you."

"Let me see some ID," said the bartender. He puffed out his chest.

She reached into her cleavage and pulled out her identification card. Her smile alone was enough to make Bryan and the bartender sweat.

The bartender looked at her photo and was surprised that the DMV allowed her to take a picture with all her white and black makeup.

"I know," she said. "I don't look my age."

"I can't seem to find your age on this card."

"You have your thumb over it, silly." She laughed. Her fingers pushed back a lock of hair behind her ear and exposed her neck to Bryan.

"What's… um… your name?"

"Why do you want to know my name?"

The drunk lad could not find the words. He just stared at her lips and imagined his lips on them.

"Her name is Omi," interrupted the bartender.

"Omi who… um?"

"It just says Omi. Where is your age?"

Omi put her head down and looked up at Bryan, who had to wipe the spit off his bottom lip. He was drooling.

"There's a good boy," she said, petting Bryan's head. "It's on there."

*****

"Why do you prefer the red pill?" asked Todd. He did not have a choice, but to ask questions.

"I thought you'd never ask," responded Professor Tinman. When he snapped his fingers, a crystal ball appeared between the gentlemen. It floated in midair and made a faint whistling sound as it spun. "You're a used man. You have been conditioned from the day you were born to be a hero to mankind. Let me ask you this, Todd Baitmen. When your wife divorced you, did you question your existence? Did you ever ask yourself, what is the whole point of love if you are going to be disposed of later in life? Whose life are you living?"

A family portrait of him appeared in the crystal ball. It was in the beginning, when his step kids were only one and two years of age. It felt like a knife went into his heart when he recalled the memories of the breakup.

Todd only blinked in confusion. He was confused about what little he knew about his situation. How did this skeleton man know his deepest darkest secrets?

"The red pill is reality. You get to see the man behind the curtain. Instead of avoiding conflict, you go through conflict to achieve what you need to make your life meaningful. You do not need female validation. In fact, you'll never allow a woman to burn you ever again."

"Sometimes, evil comes in the shape of a woman. Even though I do not like to admit it, I'm thankful for the Hell, I went through when I was with her."

"They have to hate you before they can respect you."

Professor Tinman did not give Todd time to answer. The skull painted man went on a tangent about the red pill, he even pulled a glowing red pill from his pocket and held it in the left palm of his left hand.

"Are you willing to see how the world views you? My heart was broken when I saw what I have become. Why do they see me like this? All I wanted to do was be in love with her, but the truth is, I was weak. She left me because I cut my hair and lost all my strength. That's a bible reference and a poetic way of saying that I was unworthy."

*****

"You're such a good little boy, give Momma kisses," said Omi.

The bartender stopped looking for her age, because what he saw happen before his eyes, made him urinate in his pants.

Bryan was transforming and shrinking right before his eyes. The protestors outside continued to scream, block traffic, and wave their signs. They were right outside and did not witness the horror inside.

A puppy dog was hanging from the scruff oh his neck in Omi's hand. He looked cute and innocent. Now, Bryan

the puppy even licked the fingertips of Omi's black colored
nail polish.

Suddenly, she grasped the small head of the pup and
gave it a hard twist. She looked the bartender in the eyes as
there was a disgusting popping sound. The sound the dead
dog made when she dropped it on the counter, caused the
bartender to drop her ID card and throw up all over the floor.

He uttered one word before running out of the bar,
"Witch."

The bartender would have run to the hills if it weren't
for the large protesting. He was looking for any sort of space
that would allow him to escape the woman named Omi.

"He's a misogynist! He's a racist!" screamed the pale
faced woman.

Before the bartender could respond, a protester swung a
skateboard right into the middle of his forehead. Cutting
him wide open and killing him instantly. Other protests
stomped on his lifeless corpse.

"Now let's burn down this bigot's business!" demanded
Omi.

That was the start of many fires. Local business burned
to the ground and it made her laugh.

*****

"What if I don't want to take the red pill?" asked Todd.

"There is another pill. It is this one," Professor Tinman
responded. He pulled out a black pill and held it between
his thumb and pointer finger of his right hand.

"What will happen if I take that one?"

"Few have taken this one," said Professor Tinman. "When you take this one, you completely cut out all distractions in your life."

Todd raised an eyebrow. The look on the professor's face showed that he was going to explain the effects that the black pill will have if consumed.

"Every man has a dream. A dream of riches, fame, and fortune," he said. "However, it is almost impossible to achieve with the distraction of a woman's love. If you don't do certain tasks, she'll leave you. If you say certain things, she'll leave you. It turns a man's soul to black."

"Once they are burned by a woman, they one hundred percent cut women out of their lives. It can be a bit radical, where they smirk silently, when they hear of women abuse and women killings. They are shamed by the mob by being called gay or misogynists. Despite all that, they live free and rich lives."

Todd sat in silence for a moment, pondering the meaning of what the professor said.

"So, what will it be?" he asked. "The red, or the black?"

"Didn't you say there was a fourth?"

*****

Professor Tinman was taken aback. He forgot that there was the fourth. "There is a fourth pill, the purple pill, but I strongly recommend that you don't ask me about it."

"Tell me about the fourth pill," pressed Todd.

If it wasn't so dark in the tent and the professor wasn't wearing makeup, he could see that he was sweating. Todd coughed and it made him jump.

"Fine! I'll tell you," he said. "I'll tell you, but I won't show you. When you take the purple pill, it is mixing the awareness of the red pill, with the fantasy world of the blue pill. Once you go red pill, you can never go back. You can't go back to being blue pill either. You must commit to one or the other."

"Why do you have the purple pill if you aren't able to take it?" asked Todd. His fear of the unknown was transforming into confidence. The kind of confidence you get when you are negotiating with ignorant people.

The skeleton man was looking nervous. It would be the first time somebody pressed him for the purple pill.

"Knowledge is power. I will never do the purple pill, because it damages your thinking and will eventually lead to chaos and bloodshed. A giant percentage of deaths come about with murder and suicide, but at random. The speed at which these things happen, is amplified. It is like getting on the freeway with your bad intentions. People die on the inside and then people die on the outside. It is radical. Please do not take the purple pill."

"What about my children?"

The professor's eyes glowed red and the crystal ball in front of Todd began to swirl around and around, until it showed three little girls and a woman, Caroline.

"When can we see our dad again?"

"Sweetie, that isn't your dad."

"Yes, he is!" said the youngest child. She began to cry.

"Please don't make it harder than it already is. Now we can start over and get you a new and better daddy."

"I don't want another daddy; I want my daddy."

"Your daddy doesn't care about you."

"Don't say that!"

The older daughter crossed her arms and listened to Caroline speak. The middle child cried, silently. *"Listen my love. I did not want any of this to happen. I wanted us to feel secure and that way I can raise you three the best way that I can. If he changed, I might be able to bring him back. Would you like it if he can back?"*

She nodded her head.

"Stop crying and let us go home." She let out a breath and took her daughter by the hand.

*****

His eyes returned to normal. If being a skeleton man with white eyes were normal.

"Why did you show me that?" asked Todd.

"It was an example. The thoughts that are going through your head, must be a random toss between good and evil." The purple pill amplifies those thoughts.

"Was that the future?"

"It is the present."

Todd scoffed and leaned back in his chair and crossed his arms.

"What will it be? Then you can go." As soon as the professor stopped talking, the flap of the tent opened and let in the daylight and the smell of smoke in the air.

A moment went by. Todd looked at the skeleton man, then at the red pill. The red pill is what he recommended.

The black pill would isolate him completely, but then he looked at the blue pill on the table.

The professor moved forward without saying anything, indicating that he had his say and it is now the time to choose.

It was his stepdaughter he saw in the mirror that caused him to do what he was about to do next. Without warning and with such velocity, Todd reached up and grabbed the red pill and the blue pill form the table, then ran toward the entrance.

"No!" screamed Professor Tinman. "I wouldn't do that!"

The only response he got, was the faint footsteps of Todd running down the alley way.

*****

Todd's dad sat in a recliner that was too close to the television set. He was going deaf and could not hear what was being said about the protests that were going on his community. He had a skinny metal end-table next to him that had his ashtray and whisky on it.

His cigarette was lit and giving of a stream of smoke as it rested on the side of the ashtray, so he could pour himself another drink. When he lifted the bottle over the glass, the front door swung open hard, causing him to drop the bottle all over the floor.

"Dagnabbit!" he reached leaning over the arm of his recliner and picked up the bottle before it was completely emptied out onto the carpet. "You're lucky, I didn't pull my gun out on you. They're burning buildings now, all of it caught on camera."

"Um… sorry," said Todd. "The streets are covered with people. I had to walk here. I'll have to pick up my car tomorrow."

"That's if they leave. They have been protesting for over three months in Portland. I never thought I would see something like this in my lifetime." Todd's dad finally poured himself a full glass of whiskey, finishing off the bottle. "How did court go?"

Todd scoffed and shut the door. He had his fist clutched tightly in a fist and it was behind his back. "How do you think it went?"

"Don't tell me she took everything from you."

His son remained silent.

"It must run in the family. Your mother pulled that crap, and got everything, including you. Then she packed up all her stuff and skipped town. The paperwork was a nightmare, but you were worth it."

"Thanks, Dad," said Todd, awkwardly. "I have to use the bathroom."

*****

Todd locked the bathroom door behind himself and looked in the mirror. He did not like his reflection one bit. All that was going to change.

He opened his fists and revealed the two neon pills in his palm. The red one and the blue one.

Nobody was going to tell him what to do from this day forth. He was going to use the awareness of the red pill and use it to go back to Fantasyland that the blue pill offered. Maybe then, he would be reunited with his children that were torn away from him. Torn away because his ex-wife changed her mind.

There was a glass on the bathroom counter that his dad must have forgotten to take into the kitchen. His father's drinking had begun to get a little out of control. Todd filled it up with the cold tap water. He threw back the pills and drank the whole glass of water.

I want to see how the world perceives me, thought Todd.

It took about thirty seconds, before his stomach began to feel like it was on fire. Was it water that he drank, or was it sulfuric acid? It hurt his insides.

His body was transforming right before his eyes.

There were chills all over his body, but he felt like he was being burned alive from the inside. His arm jerked and hit the bathroom light switch. The lights went out in the bathroom and he let out a giant roar.

*****

Todd's dad lit his cigarette, but almost burned himself when he heard a roar coming from the other side of the house. He reached over and picked up the remote to the television and pressed MUTE.

"Todd?" he asked. "You better not have brought a cat into this house. You know I'm allergic to pussycat-dandruff. It'll clog up my lungs and suffocate me."

He took a hard drag off his cigarette and could not help a smile. The irony that he was afraid to breath in cat particles, but not afraid to fill his lungs up with smoke.

There was no answer from his son. He was interrupted by the lights shutting off completely throughout the house. Only the cherry at the end of his cigarette could be seen in the darkness.

"What is going on? The protesters better not come in my neighborhood. I will show them a thing or two. I got my piece, right here?"

A 45 Smith and Wesson was pulled out of its holster and cocked back. The sound of it would be enough to scare away any intruder if they dare enter unwelcomed.

"Achoo!" sneezed Todd's dad. "I mean it, Todd. You better not have brought home any pussycats, otherwise I will have to shoot them. Dagnabbit! I burned a hole in the carpet!"

A small flame emerged from the carpet, but Todd's dad quickly stomped it out. It was enough of a distraction, that he did not see the pair of glowing purple eyes behind him.

He sneezed again. The eyes in the night, were stalking him as he went over to the living room window to let in the light from the streetlamp. When he pulled back the curtain and turned around. He came face to face with the purple eyes and the teeth below them.

*****

The creature was wearing Todd's clothes, only they hung off of its body in rags. Like the Incredible Hulk. The claws were huge and the tips of them sparkled as the light hit them. A tail could be seen wagging behind him. The feet matched his claws.

53

Todd's dad tried to scream, but he was hit with a sneezing attack. It was not enough to stop him from reaching for his firearm. He lifted the cannon up and pointed it at the monster.

The monster's claw reached out and gripped the man's gun, hand, and forearm in crushed it. It made sickening squish sound. Now Todd's dad screamed in agony and horror. The teeth chomped at his neck and was easily removed, and it slid down the cat-creature's mouth.

Todd threw his head back and roared again.

The bloody corpse lay at Todd's feet. There was no mouth, no neck, and no chest left of Todd's dad. Still, a black neon pill was able to fall out of the dead body. Todd was oblivious to it but jumped through the window. Glass flew in all direction.

He took off running on all fours down the street.

*****

The neighbor patted his cat on the head. It walked across his computer screen and pressed a bunch of keys, messing up what he had just written.

"You know I'm not going to get anything done with you doing that."

The cat only meowed at him.

"Is that your way of telling me, to go fuck myself?" laughed the neighbor.

Other cats were rubbing against his leg and purring. It was helping him stay in the groove of writing, until he was rudely interrupted by the cat on his keyboard.

"Would you like me to tell you about the story I'm writing?"

"Meow."

"It's about a girl," the neighbor went on. "I know, I know, no love stories. It's the horror stories that pay the bills, but it's this one that's going to make me a fortune, because it's based on a true story."

"Meow?"

"I don't know if I should tell you right now. You might get scared."

"Hiss!"

Suddenly, all the cats were hissing. Some of them clawed themselves to his pant legs. The cat on his keyboard swiped at the air.

"What is it?" asked the neighbor. He looked over his shoulder and saw two purple eyes and teeth.

*****

Before the neighbor could scream, he was backhanded out of his chair and shoes by the giant claw of the monster. He hit the wall.

Instantly, the neighbor's left arm was broken. He had a wound on his head because blood was pouring into his right eye. With his left, he could see the cat-creature standing over him.

"You, you stupid idiot!" he screamed in pain. "You took the purple pill. How could you? The professor warned you not to do it. Look what you have done!"

Todd did not know if he could speak. The teeth took up most of the room in his mouth, but he tried it and it worked. "Where's Caroline? Where are my kids?"

"How should I know?" said the neighbor. "I don't give a fuck about you, or your wife. You ruined my life's work. Look at my arm!"

"You two were lovers and all she had to do was get rid of me. Admit it."

The neighbor looked at Todd with a grotesque and confused look. He shifted his weight and was able to sit up.

"It's all about status in this world and you're the only one who's capable of pulling something like this."

"You're not thinking straight! It's the purple pill!"

The cat's continued to hiss at Todd. Todd looked at them with his purple eyes and hissed back. One of the cats passed out from and keeled over on the floor.

"Admit it! You're trying to tear my family apart."

*****

There was a window of opportunity for the neighbor. He too was about to pass out from the pain and the inconvenience, but then Todd looked through the window and peered into his old residence.

The house was dark but standing inside his old bedroom with her arms crossed, was a girl covered in tattoos. She was smiling at him.

Who is she? How come she's staring at me like that? BANG! BANG! BANG!

*****

The neighbor shot Todd in the neck; he pulled his firearm from a holster attached to his ankle. The cat-creature held his neck and meowed in pain.

Todd fell to his knees and then hit the ground hard. Todd uttered some words before he died. "What pill did you take?"

The purple color left Todd's eyes and a neon purple pill fell out of his mouth.

"None of your business."

The Emerald Child

The sounds of gunfire broke through the desert air. Bullets peppered a wooden door, trying to kill the person behind it with no success. The gunfire belonged to large creatures clothed in black robes and golden headdresses. There were two dozen of them trying to complete their task given to them by their master.

Some carried clubs and a few wielded swords. They waited behind the others who were blasting their pistols and shotguns. They screamed a battle cry at the top of their lungs.

A man named Castor was holding his position behind the door. Every few minutes he would return fire to the golden demons. He cursed them and their master while he reloaded his guns.

"You golden vermin! The lot of you!" Castor emptied his magazine through a hole in the door and finally struck one in the shoulder. The sound the creature let out could spoil milk.

When he went to reach for ammo in his side purse, he found that there was not enough ammo for them all. If he did not shoot back, the cloaked figures would know that he was empty and would swarm him.

The small house he was in had a giant hole in it. Thank goodness the creatures did not notice it, otherwise the ones with the swords would be able to flank him. Caster looked out of a hole and saw the creatures throwing rocks at the building, trying to weaken the door. The door was going to give way any second.

He shot one bullet to every ten they shot at him. Soon he was left with four shots. Just then he felt a tug on his pant leg and with a sudden move he had a pistol shoved under his chin.

"Take it easy partner, it's only me," said Inquisitor Telemon. "I knew if I followed the sounds of killing, I would find you."

"Where's the robot?"

"Who? TAO-38? I do not know. He was supposed to be opening that metal door a few blocks over. I told him that I was going to get you…"

"Are you ever going to shut up?" said Caster, cutting off Telemon. He grabbed the ammo purse that was around Telemon's waist. He too was carrying guns on his sides and a short sword was in its scabbard.

Before Caster could tell Telemon that the robot better have the door open soon. A club crashed through the door, bringing in the first cloaked figure. Castor and Telemon both fell over backwards, dumping their bag of ammo all over the floor.

Telemon quickly recovered and pulled out his sword. He dodged another swing of the club and was able to cut the side of the vermin. It did not do much to stop another swing at him, but Telemon was a small man and that was making him a hard target to hit.

Three cloaked swordsmen came in and focused on Castor who picked up his hat from the dirt. He shot one in the gut and ducked in time to save the marriage between his head and his shoulders. This would be one of many times during this attack that he came close to death.

Fear was trying to creep into Castor's mind. That was what these creatures did. They drove fear into the hearts of men with every appearance and stroke of their weapons. Doubt in oneself kills a man when dealing with demons like these.

The creature that Telemon was wrestling with had finally made a wrong move and was dealt a killing blow to the neck. When one cloaked figure fell, another took its place. The cloaked swordsman had taken a frustrated swing at Caster only to miss again and chopped off his partner's head. The body crashed to the floor like a puppet with its strings cut.

This may have been avoided if Caster did not sneak into the black castle and steal the master's treasure. The Emerald Child.

He Rang

Howie could not sleep. It had been twenty-four hours since his girlfriend, Morgan, packed up her things and left. *Is she really gone? Am I in denial?* After a while, he admitted to himself that he was spending more time playing video games, than spending time with his girlfriend. A three-year relationship down the drain, all because he couldn't stop playing. Howie had grown complacent.

His bed felt like laying on a raft in the middle of the ocean with no rescue in sight. The room was pitch black. Despite being almost thirty years old, Howie was afraid of the dark. He never told Morgan, but because of her, he found courage.

The house was five miles from the closest town. A big house with a staircase and giant windows. It was too big for the two of them and now it felt like a prison. She left while he was at work. It took fifteen minutes to realize that her stuff was missing, and he knew instantly why Morgan left. It was because he was not paying any attention to her when he got home. He went straight from being home, to sitting and playing his game until it was bedtime.

He thought that if he got rid of it, that it may fix some of the problem. Howie ripped it out of the wall and heaved it into the dumpster across the street, under the streetlamp.

Now that it was trashed, he believed the universe would tell Morgan that he 'saw the errors of his ways' and would force her to come back. This did not work at all. Now he lay in the dark in fear. A fear that he deserved to have for neglecting his girlfriend's needs.

Sleep almost came, but a light from outside shined through the bedroom window. Howie got up and looked through the window and saw the game console shining in the streetlamp. If the console could speak, it might ask to be lifted out of the garbage and be plugged back inside the house.

What if she never came back? She is being a little dramatic. She knows that I play a lot and said that she was okay with it.

He thought hard and stared at the game console protruding out of the trash. Should he go and get it? Maybe *he* was being a bit dramatic. Then all of a sudden, a vibrating sound could be heard. It was the sound of metal vibrating on wood. He jumped with a panic induced spasm at the sudden break in silence. He quickly calmed himself when he realized it was his phone ringing on the end table. A moment of excitement gripped him as the hoped it was Morgan. Picking up his phone, he was eager to answer.

An unknown phone number was displayed across the screen. A scoff of disappointment, Howie was always taught never to answer such calls, so he pressed the END

CALL button. *It could be Morgan's sister testing me*, he thought. She would support Morgan and would try and play mind games with him. A test to see if Howie would beg for her to come back. He already called and left a bunch of messages and that ate up his battery. It was after he filled her voicemail Howie began to feel like a creep.

The feeling of being creepy and unattractive, kept Howie in a constant state of anxiety, the anxiety made it so. Watching television would be therapeutic and while he was watching it, he could come up with a solution. Baby steps. When he pressed the POWER button, there was not a reaction. He pressed it once more and the same result occurred.

It was plugged in.

There was not a reaction when Howie flipped the switch that would turn on the light in his room. The room remained black, except for the light from the streetlamp. Maybe there was a power outage at his house only.

Damn it!

He turned the flashlight on; on his phone and went downstairs to the power box. When he found the box, Howie noticed that his phone only had five percent left of battery life. There was no way he was going to be able to charge his phone, if he did not get the house back up to par.

When he checked the power box, nothing seemed out of the ordinary. Howie tried all the switches and found that no matter how many times, or how long he switched them on and off, that the power box wasn't going to produce electricity. He would have to call an electrician, but there was no one available this late at night. It would have to wait until morning.

His phone vibrated in his hand, nearly making him drop it. It was the same unknown number.

"Hello?" answered Howie. His heart was pounding in his chest from anxiety. "Hello? Morgan, is this you?"

"*I see you in the window,*" said a man's voice.

"I'm sorry, I think you have the wrong number."

"*No wrong number,*" he said. "*I see you at the window. I want you to let me in the house.*"

"Don't call this number ever again," said Howie. He was trying to sound tough, but it came out as a whine. His thumb ended the call before the person could say another word.

As soon as he hung up, the phone began to ring again. "I said to stop calling me or I'll call the police!"

"*Call me, they won't make it in time. I haven't seen a car in hours.*"

That sent shivers down Howie's spine, "What do you want?"

"*Let me in the house. I used to live there.*"

"How stupid do you think I am?"

There was a sudden rustle on the roof. Howie ducked down to the floor. His lungs and groin started to hurt, from holding his breath and urine.

There was laughter on the other end of the phone. "*I see you get scared, it was so funny, they're cats on your roof.*"

The voice on the other line must be close; to see on top of the roof. "Where are you?"

"Look past the streetlamp, I'm only a few yards from that."

He got to his feet and looked out the window. The amount of strain he put on his eyes to see past the lamp, made his eyes hurt. Howie saw a giant humanoid figure. Its arm rest on top of a payphone box. Morgan would always comment about it, saying that it was outdated and needed to be removed.

He flicked his lighter and the flame from it; revealed his face. It was a horrific face.

"Don't I look pretty?"

*****

"I think you might be a little hard on him," said Charlie. She was sitting across from her sister. Morgan's phone was laying in the middle of the wooden coffee table, with missed calls from Howie. "He's called almost a hundred times."

Morgan did not say a word. She just watching television like a robot, not listening to anything Howie related.

"If you're not going to listen to your messages, can I listen to them?"

"Go ahead. I'm sure he can survive one night without me."

*****

The giant at the payphone was hairy. His hair and beard were dark red and thick, like a nest of red worms and snakes. His face was painted white and his nose missing. The hole where it needed to be, was painted black.

Those features were not what scared Howie the most. It was his teeth. Huge teeth that made the giant clown smile with bright cruelty.

"If you hang up this phone on me again. I'll marry you with this." The clown brought out a small double-bladed ax from behind him, tauntingly.

*****

Charlie had finished a few of the messages that Howie left. Morgan looked like she was frozen in time. She did not care that her sister was going through her private messages. Her eyes were glued to the television. The two sisters were watching The Voice and there were a few love songs that almost got Morgan teary eyed, but she stayed strong.

"Morgan, you have to call him," said Charlie, letting her emotions get the best of her. "He sounds like he's genuinely sorry for being an asshole."

"Let me guess," spoke Morgan, finally. "He sent me a long message saying he loves me, he's sorry, and he threw his game away."

"Pretty spot-on sis, how did you know?"

"This isn't our first fight!" Morgan exploded like a shaken soda pop. "You have no idea how many times I've come home from work, just to find him sitting on his butt playing video games. He never asks me about my day or anything like that. Howie cares only about Howie."

"I know that must be rotten," said Charlie sarcastically "You know men are like that. Have you ever tried to play some of the games with him?"

Morgan looked away and slowly shook her head. "I guess I never thought of it that way before."

"Sometimes we make dramatic decisions when we're mad." Charlie shrugged her shoulders.

Morgan rolled her eyes, "I'll give him a call."

*****

"Look dude, my phone is about to die," said Howie, frozen in place at the window. The clown was doing an amazing job of keeping him on the phone. "I gotta go. Please let me go."

"I will have no choice but to take back my house by force," said the clown. *"I didn't think it through when I cut the electricity."*

Howie's worrying and anxiety was interrupted by his own thoughts, if he didn't calm down, he would most certainly have a panic attack. *Is this really happening? What are you going to do Howie? You can call the police with the little battery you have left and get help. Maybe there is police car in the neighborhood. What about the neighborhood watch?*

What if he gets inside the house before you can tell the police your address? Are you willing to take that risk? Make a choice already!

He ended the call. It was already taking too long for Howie to dial 911. He pressed the number nine and that was when he heard the clown drop the phone. It swayed back and forth and hung there dead.

*****

"It went straight to voice mail," said Morgan. She looked at her phone puzzled. "Maybe *he's* mad at me."

"I doubt that he's mad at you. He was leaving messages for you all day," said Charlie.

"We interrupt this program to give warning of an escaped patient from the Oregon State Asylum. An escapee that has left officials scratching their heads. With around the clock supervision, patient Ian Zane was able to walk out of the building without detection. Your local police department will give safety tips on how to stay safe."

"Here is a photo of the patient known as Ian Zane. Police say he might have altered his appearance. If you see him, let the authorities know right away. Do not approach, do not provoke, and above all else, do not speak to this man."

"He looks like an absolute nutcase." The picture showed Ian smiling. His eyes looked like they could cut ribbons and his long pointy nose poked out like a spike. It was the patient's teeth that haunted Morgan. They were giant teeth and they looked like they did not fit in his head. His teeth gave him an evil grin.

The photo did nothing but creep the pants off the two girls.

"He's out there and Howie is all alone," said Morgan. Her hands went over her mouth, because of how worried she was.

"Howie is going to be fine," said Charlie. "He might like video games a little too much, but I don't think he's dumbed enough to forget to lock his doors."

Morgan did not listen to what her sister was saying. "I just wish he'd answer his phone."

*****

Howie's first intention was to run to the garage and drive away, except that would not work because of the power being cut. There would be no way to open the garage door. He was trying to be smart about the whole situation, but he was doubting his ability to survive. The clown could be seen through the glass sliding doors and when the clown came into the light, the ax looked cartoonish because of how shiny and sharp it was.

How was he going to fight him off? He had no weapon and it was still pitch black in the house. Howie was planted and shaky and just watched the clown come closer and closer to the glass door with the ax. The size of the clown blocked the streetlamp and that was enough to get Howie's legs moving upstairs.

A crash came from downstairs. It was the sound of glass breaking and wood splitting. Crunching sounds of the clown's feet walking over the glass and breaking it. Then it was quiet for a few seconds, but then there was the sound of a bic being flicked.

The bic had lit a ball of light for the clown to search five inches in front of him. It moved around like a phantom light. To be spotted, would mean the end for Howie.

*****

The closet had everything in it, except a weapon. Howie was lucky the clown was carrying an ax and not a gun. *Or does he have one concealed?*

He was going to have to go out the window and be out and on top of the roof. Howie grabbed the bottom of the window and jerked it upwards but injured his fingers because the window was locked. While Howie was shaking the pain away, the ball of light was almost at the top of the stairs and so were the heavy footsteps. *Here he comes! You better hurry! Unlock the window and get the heck out of here. Have you ever felt an ax in the back?*

*****

Howie screamed like a little girl. Not because he felt the blade dig into his back, but because he had successfully opened the window and had half his body out already. He was escaping with his life. One knee was up, and he was about to do a push up that would get him to his feet, but he felt the cold steel in his calf.

If he did not get his foot out with the rest of his body, the clown would have successfully cut it off. That was not the case, but there was blood everywhere and Howie was surprised that he could walk with a limp toward the satellite dish on the roof.

Will the clown be able to fit through the window? Was he safe with only the one injury?

That was when the giant clown, with one swing of his ax, was able to create a hole big enough for him to pass through. Howie didn't know if the clown was laughing, or if the alien sound was coming from the hole in the clown's face. Perhaps it was a bit of both.

"Get out of my house!" yelled the clown though his titanic teeth.

*****

The satellites cord was loose, and Howie ripped it from the metal bracings on the side of the house. The dish was mounted with four bolts, making it strong enough for him to swing down to safety. There was still a fighting chance he would get out of this alive!

He could hear those heavy footsteps. Howie wrapped the cord around his hands and threw himself off the roof. He did fall from the roof, but not before the ax struck his shoulder. It about tore him in half! His vision blurred from the pain. The added momentum caused him to spin, and the cord wrapped around his neck, catching him right before he hit the ground.

The clown looked at Howie in shock and amazement. The clown drove the axe into the side of roof, leaning on the handle, Ian Zane pulled out his cigarettes and placed one between his gnarly teeth. It was on the third try that the giant clown was able to light his cig, because he could not help but laugh at what happened. Smoke came billowing out of the fresh hole in the center of his face.

*****

The next morning, Morgan and Charlie drove their dad's truck to Howie's house. They took their dad's truck, so they could use that as an excuse to leave. They would say that they needed to go because their dad needed his truck back if the conversation between Howie and Morgan went sour.

"What are you going to say to him?" asked Charlie.

Morgan shrugged her shoulders and did not give an answer to her sister's question. Instead, she glanced over at the phone booth that was so near to their house. Seeing it gave her a bad feeling and she just wanted somebody to get rid of it already. Some weirdo must have used it because the receiver was hanging by the cord.

When the sisters arrived at the house only a moment later, they got out of the truck and froze. Howie was hanging from the roof much like payphone receiver.

Morgan began sobbing. "My Howie."

Shavings

"How come you don't ask out the deli girl?" asked Ronald. He poked his coworker in the side with his pointer finger. "She's hot and you need a rebound."

Eli did not say a word and cut open a case of Spanish Rice to stock the shelf. "I don't want to talk about girls right now. I have the worst luck with girls anyways."

"Come on," said Ronald. "She's new in town and even though she looks emo, I think you two would make a great couple. Just look at her."

He could not look at her, because it would remind him of the breakup. Ronald grabbed his arm and jerked him away from the grocery shelf and faced him toward the girl standing behind the counter.

Eli saw her and froze. She was leaning on her right hand and tapping the counter with the left.

Her hair was black and so was her nail polish. She wore one pigtail on the right side of her head, resembling some sort of anime character.

"Look at the time," said Ronald. He put his hands-on Eli's shoulders and pushed him toward her. "You look like you need a sandwich, Eli. Would you mind making one?"

Eli's face turned bright red, because Ronald said it loud enough that she was able to hear him, Ronald then walked away. She raised her eyebrow in confusion and then looked at Eli.

The silence was deafening. The girl behind the counter started to look like she was going to run away in fear. Before she could do anything, Eli finally opened his mouth. "May I have a sandwich?"

"What do I look like? Your mother?" she asked.

Eli began to sweat. *What should I say after this?*

"I'm just kidding. I will fix you up something. Do you like bologna?"

He nodded. *If we were the last people on Earth, she would kill herself before being with me,* he thought to himself.

She wrote the order down on a sticky note and stuck it on the metal shelf, that way she could read it. Her clothes covered her arms and her neck. Her eyes were a beautiful blue; causing him to stare.

"Is that everything for you?" She looked at him and scrunched her eyebrows together.

Once she spoke, Eli snapped out of his daze and shook his head. "I'm sorry. I do not know what just happened… um… are you new in… um… town?"

"Today would make five days," she said. "I'm a fast learner. Do not be fooled by me. Even though I just moved here, doesn't mean I know what everyone is up to." Omi pushed his sandwich in front of him.

His wallet was in his back pocket, but when he went to reach for it. She put her hand up and interrupted him, "Don't worry, it's on me."

"You don't have to do that," said Eli. Her act of kindness made him feel uncomfortable.

"Just because I am new in town, doesn't mean I don't have any money. You're just going to have to take me out tonight."

"I don't even know your name." His eyes were gigantic.

"My name's Omi."

*****

Eli did not see Omi for the rest of the day. He told Ronald all the details, "I told you'd find a new girl. No more of that other one."

Now he was in his bathroom, combing his hair. Omi was going to be off work in an hour. She told him that she was going to meet him at La Flama Mexican Restaurant, and not to be late. With the constant anxiety—fueled by the fear of his attire—and thinking of what he is going to say to her on the date, his past breakup was now in the back of his mind.

He thought about her all the time and there was nothing he could do. Eli did not think anyone would like him like that ever again. It hurt for a long time. Every day for six months, his ex was on his mind, but not now.

Eli decided on a look that he thought she might like. That was a black t-shirt and blue jeans. He tipped the bottle of cologne into his palm and put it under his armpits, around his neck, and put a drop in the front of his pants.

He bought some roses at a small gift shop, right next to the Restaurant. Twelve roses were tied together with a red ribbon. They looked and felt so delicate, that when Eli put them in the car, he buckled them up in the passenger-seat.

She told him that she got off at six and would be an hour. Eli parked his car in the back of the building and got out of the car. He took a napkin from his backseat and wiped the sweat protruding from his forehead.

His watch read 7:05 and instantly, is his flight-or-fight system was going awry. He felt almost lightheaded when he walked up to the front door. Eli counted to ten and took two deep breaths.

What if she does not show up? What if she is already here? Do I kiss her? Do I make a move? Is kissing her making a move?

"There you are!" said a girl's voice through the crack of an ajar metal door. "I got us a booth in the bar section."

Eli screamed and opened his eyes. He saw the door swing shut. *Was that Omi?*

*****

The bar was to the left. If he heard her correctly, she was waiting for him in the bar. Eli had only been twenty-one for only a couple months and had yet to set foot in a bar. When he did, she was sitting in a red booth and she looked like a ghost.

Her face was painted white and her lipstick was black. It made Omi's teeth look like they were glowing white light and her tongue was a crimson ribbon. Neck, shoulders, and wrists were exposed. She was covered from head-to-toe in tattoos. Black and gray. No other colors, except for her blue eyes.

Omi resembled a beautiful clown. If clowns could be considered beautiful.

"These are for you," said Eli. Shoving the flowers at her with such force, that the roses lost some pedals.

"Oh… thanks," she said, taking them from him. "You… um… you can sit down."

Eli sat down and quickly picked up a menu.

The waitress came over and Eli could hear her and his date whispering to each other. Eli looked over the top of his menu and both girls stopped their chatter and looked at him.

"May I take your order?" asked the waitress.

His heart was pounding in his chest. This was the same waitress that waited on him and his ex-girlfriend. What could she be thinking of him?

"What would you like to eat?" he asked Omi. His voice cracked. The waitress held her laugh.

"You order first," said Omi. She did not want to be rude like the waitress.

"Um… I… uh… would like the chicken tacos, please. Is that okay?"

"We can share," said Omi, helping. She took the menu from Eli and handed it to the waitress. "Thanks."

*****

After she brought them their food and drinks, Omi finally took pity on Eli and spoke to him. "You haven't been on a date in a long time. Am I right?"

He thought this girl must like him, if she was still here after all the silence and awkwardness. Eli nodded and he was red in the face.

"I can tell," she said, smiling. "It's because of your ex?"

Eli's eyes twisted in a horrific shape. *How the hell did she know?*

Omi giggled. "Would you believe me if I told you; my previous job I was a fortune teller?" She didn't allow Eli to respond. "The waitress told me too. I know you do not like to talk about it, because you think about her all the time. You might as well tell me. Give me your hand."

She reached over and took his hand. Eli felt as though his head might explode. He had not felt a woman's touch since a good while before the breakup. It made him feel warm and fuzzy inside. Omi was reading his palm.

"Her name is Alexia," she said.

How did she know? thought Eli. He listened to her while she traced the lines in the middle of his hand.

"She told you something that haunts your dreams. Alexia made the statement that you've never done anything challenging in your life." Omi did not have to look at him to know she was right.

"Alexia took you for granted. She used you for your time and your money. If she didn't have it her way, she would shame you into spending money that you didn't have." Eli tensed up hearing his truth coming from her mouth.

"You think all women are this way. You have been burned and you are just done with all of us and you are going your own way. You blame yourself for everything and take offense when people call you a nice guy."

Omi let go of his hand. "You can't tell under my makeup, but I'm blushing. You were burned by women, but you still asked me out."

"I did?" asked Eli. She put a hand up to this mouth, in disbelief. He didn't remember asking her out, but there is the risk of offending her, so he lied, "I mean, I did. You're the exception." They sat and ate their dinner.

"Walk me home, Eli."

"Right now?" he asked.

Omi nodded. She pulled out a fifty-dollar bill and slammed it on the table. "I live at the end of main street."

*****

They walked out of La Flama and down the dark street, toward Omi's house. Eli never walked down this part of town before. Due to the rumors of gangs.

There is a first for everything. First the breakup and now he was looking at the black house that belong to the pale faced girl, Omi.

"Beautiful, isn't it?" she said. Both looked up at the house, "Most people are afraid of it, but I love it."

"This house?" asked Eli. He couldn't believe what he just said out loud, "I didn't mean it like that. It is just this house has been abandoned for years. Everyone knows it's haunted."

"That's why I bought it. So far, I haven't seen anything strange, but I do have something for you. I feel it will help you get over yourself. I call it unworthiness," Omi squeezed Eli's hand and whispered in his ear. She told him, "Wait right here."

Eli twiddled his thumbs and thought to himself. *You are supposed to kiss girls at the end of a date.* If he did not, how else is she going to know that he likes her?

The sound of Omi's door opening back up, was enough to snap Eli out of his fantasy. She was hiding something behind her back.

Eli came close to Omi and went in for the kiss. Before he could kiss her black lipstick-stained lips, she shoved what she had behind her back into his arms. It was a black, rectangular box.

"What's this?"

She avoided his question, "I'll tell you what. You take this home and do what it says on the paper in the box, and I'll have you over for a night you'll never forget," said Omi with a wink.

"I don't understand," he said. The box was heavy in his hands.

"Let me be clear. If you take this home and do what it says on the paper, I'll sleep with you."

Eli grabbed the box.

"Okay, I'll give it a try." He smiled awkwardly. Omi then gave him a quick kiss on the cheek and walked back into the house.

*****

Eli was home now. He laid the box on top of his kitchen table and sat on the coach. *Did she really say what I thought she said? She was willing to sleep with him if he played with whatever was in the box?*

He thought about calling Ronald and telling him about the date and her proposition. Except the box was sticking out like a sore thumb. Eli picked up the box and placed it on the coffee table, in front of him.

It was a simple lock mechanism, which only required Eli to twist the knob and lift the lid open. Inside was a parchment. It read:

Hide and Seek

My name is Shavings and I want to play a game with you. Hide me anywhere you like and count to twenty. After you have counted, come and seek me. Once you found me, it will then be my turn. Place me in the corner and you hide. When I get to twenty...

There was nothing more. Eli thought that was odd...

*****

He reached inside the box and pulled out a small wooden marionette puppet. It had no strings attached to him. This must be Shavings.

Eli was able to stand him up on the coffee table and have a good look at him. He was a hunter, with a quiver full of arrows and a bow. They were carved right onto his body. Shaving's beard was red and thick, which made him look like a mountain man. It made Eli think of Robin Hood, only this version of him was creepier.

Was Omi really going to have sex with him if he played Hide and Seek with this puppet? Was it worth it? This sort of deal was better than the deal he got with his ex. The deal of a near sexless relationship.

There was no avoiding the feeling of stupidity, as he picked Shaving up by the arm and looked for a hiding spot. His house had only two bedrooms and a tiny bathroom.

In the spare bedroom was where Eli decided to hide him. *Under the bed! No that would be too easy. How about, on top of a shelf? No that is stupid too.*

A trunk was at the end of the bed. That would be a good place to hide Shavings. It was empty and it would be easy to find him when Eli went to go look for him.

This whole situation was strange and awkward. How would Omi know if he played with it?

While Eli was placing Shavings in the trunk. He accidentally let him slip from his fingers, because how heavy he was. On the way down, something cut Eli's finger wide open.

*****

Along with Shaving's bow and arrows, there was a small sword hidden under the sleeve of his right arm. Like an assassin's blade.

"You tricky bugger!" he said, putting his opened wound in his mouth and letting the lid shut tight.

The first aid kit was in the bathroom. That puppet's blade was razor sharp. It did not take much to cut into his fingers. He was surprised how deep it was. It took him fifteen minutes to clean the wound and dress it up.

Eli set Shavings into the trunk and shut the lid.

It was what Omi promised him that kept him playing this game. It sounded too good to be true, but it has been such a long time since he felt wanted by a woman. He made a fist with his hurt hand and went to the kitchen corner and began to count.

*****

"Ready or not! Here I come!"

Eli felt like such a fool. First, he checked behind the couch, knowing that Shavings was not back there. Then he searched the cupboards, and under the bathroom sink, yet Shaving was nowhere to be found. When he got to the trunk in the spare bedroom. He opened the box and found Shavings.

He picked him up like a baby and stood him on top of the box. This time, Shavings was eye to eye with him. Eli looked at his features and admired all details that were carved into him. Except for the eyes. The eyes were dotted on with black paint.

It was Eli's turn to hide now. He cradled Shavings and brought him to the same corner that Eli counted in. There was only one place he could hide and not feel so silly doing it.

Shavings stood like a statue in the corner. His green cape and green hat reminded Eli of a burglar he read about in books. Is there such thing as a good burglar?

"Count to twenty and I'll hurry up and hide."

*****

The dark closet in Eli's bedroom was big enough for him to hide. He shut the door quietly and sat deep inside the closet. He was a minimalist, so there was enough room for him to sit comfortably. He brought his phone with him and was about to play a game on it, but he got a text.

"How did it go?" asked Ronald.

"How did what go? The date with Omi?" replied Eli.

"Duh! You were supposed to text me how it went."

"It was interesting. That's for sure."

"Interesting? Explain now! Or I'll tell the manager that you played hooky that time Alexia broke it off with you."

"You won't do that."

"Did you get any or not?"

"I'm about to."

"What the heck does that mean?"

"She said I have to play a game before she will sleep with me."

Eli did not read what his friend wrote, because he heard something. It was not dripping water from the sink. It was not the sound of his breathing. It was the sound of something creeping on his wooden floors. He could hear footsteps walking near him.

For a second, Eli thought his hearing was going bad. He did not want to believe what was happening. If he was not mistaken, the sound of wooded footsteps was walking around in the other room.

Eli's eyes were shifting back and forth in the darkness of the closet. Eli heard it again. Wood on wood. Walking around in the living room. Talking to Ronald about being sexual with Omi, was enough to make him forget that he was playing Hide and Seek with a wooden puppet.

Was this really happening? It cannot be real. This is all a dream.

The thoughts raced through Eli's head like a bullet train. The evidence was not there to support that this was part of his imagination. It is true, the puppet named Shavings was walking around, searching for him.

When he could not take listen anymore, Eli was forced to go investigate the noise. He opened the closet door, then opened the door to his bedroom. The sound of footsteps stopped, and a shiver went up his spine.

Around the room he looked and found everything perfectly still. It was such a small apartment. It could only fit a small sofa, a coffee table, a bookshelf, a tiny television, and a recliner.

Did he interrupt Shavings seeking him?

*****

It was the front door that caught Eli's attention. The doorknob was tied with rope, to the floor with a metal ring. Eli turned the knob and pulled. It did not budge an inch. It would not move no matter how hard he pulled or pushed.

What is going on?

Eli was about to over think the situation but felt a piercing pain in his right shoulder. It burned like fire. He could see the arrowhead sticking out of his front. There was Shavings on the table, drawing another arrow. Shavings was standing inside of his box, which is why Eli did not spot him right away, the puppet hid and laid a trap.

He let loose another arrow but missed Eli by a hair. Eli was quick enough to dodge and weave, back into his bedroom.

*****

The arrow almost took out his ear. Eli slammed the door shut and inspected his shoulder further. His back was pressed hard on the door, so he could keep it shut tight, because there was no lock. The arrow was lodged in his shoulder. Eli couldn't lift his arm but could still bend his elbow… but not much. Too much bend, and his arm might fall off.

His cut on his finger was nothing compared to the pain he was feeling now.

He knew he needed to call for help. His phone was left inside of the closet. Before Eli could shift his weight to attempt to move toward the closet, Shavings' blade cut through the wooden door and into his calf. The wood that made up the door, was paper thin. A beaded curtain would have done a better job against the razor-sharp weapon.

Tears and cries erupted out of Eli.

Shavings' blade ripped out of his leg and Eli fell to the floor headfirst. Blood sprayed out of Eli's calf and painted the walls red. Blood oozed out of the arrow wound.

Surprisingly, Eli was able to use his good leg to help move him toward the closet. The blade could be seen going in and out of the wooden door, creating an entrance for the possessed puppet.

You are almost there! Do not panic! Get inside the closet and shut the door! It will buy you enough time to call for help! Pay no attention to the puppet that is trying to kill you!

Eli pulled the closet door shut. He wiped his brow with this good hand and picked up his phone. Blood began to pool below his leg. It is hard to think when your heart is beating so hard and you hear the wooden footsteps coming toward the closet door.

Eli opened his phone. He then dialed a 9' and the blade shot through the door. The blade almost went into his lower back. When Shavings went to pull the knife free from the wood, the blade got stuck.

The puppet kicked the closet door, and kept kicking it, even when Eli swung open the closet door and sandwiched Shavings between the wall and the closet door. Shavings body went limp.

*****

With one arm and one leg, Eli crawled to the bathroom and successfully made it inside. The bathroom had a lock and Eli made sure it was locked. It didn't make him feel safe, because he seen what the doll did to his apartment doors already and knew the bathroom door wasn't any different.

He had to fight back. Otherwise, he was going to die.

In the cupboard under the sink, he found some cleaning spray and a lighter in the top drawer. His apartment was on the third floor and there was a small window in the shower.

When that puppet comes through the door, he will set it on fire and toss him out the window. For how heavy the marionette is, the weight would be enough to send him out.

He began bandaging his legs as he heard footsteps outside. Shavings freed his blade from the door. Eli got on his stomach and lit the lighter.

This must work. Please! Please! Please work!

Shavings busted through the door and came through the opening.

*****

Eli squeezed the lighter and the spray can as hard as he could and was right on target. Shavings got a face full of burning death. The puppet silently shook in agony. His hat and cape caught quickly and within seconds, the doll was burning up and turning black. He smelled like burnt hair, which made Eli gag.

He finally stopped spraying. The flames danced allround the bathroom. The toilet paper and trashcan ignited. The bathroom was so small, the burning puppet was close enough to catch Eli's hair on fire.

The screams were loud enough to wake up the neighbors, outside of the apartment building.

Things were not going according to plan, Eli thought to himself.

It hurts, but you can win! You can do it! If you do not do this, you're going to die! You're going to die and Alexia will have been right about you! Prove to her that you are the prize! Survive!

Shavings arms were waving in the air and the flames were flying everywhere. Eli reached out and grabbed the puppet by leg and swung as hard as he could at the window. He plunged his head into the open toilet bowl, extinguishing his burning hair.

*****

Glass rained down into the shower and onto the ground below. Wood, fire, and glass made a satisfying sound when it hit the concrete and exploded in all directions.

Eli laid on his back and was going in and out of consciousness. His head hurt, his shoulder hurt, and his finger hurt. But his heart did not hurt anymore. When he came to, he crawled back to his bedroom and back to the closet.

He picked up his phone and tried to open it. It was tough, because his hand was fried, and it hurt to hold the phone. Eli could not help but cry again.

When he successfully opened the phone, there were missed calls and missed texts from Ronald. The first of the many messages said this:

"If you sleep with Omi, it might help get over Alexia."

*****

Omi woke from her sleep. She looked at her clock and saw that it was 3:16 AM. She thought it to be a blessing to wake up at this time. Many things happen during 3 AM. The portal to the other world is at its thinnest, perfect for the dark arts.

Before she could put on her slippers, there was another knock at the door. This time harder.

"I'm coming! I am coming! Hold your horses."

The knocking subsided.

With a match, she lit a candle and was granted orange light, revealing her room.

There was a small table in the back corner, with a crystal ball on top of it. Next to it in the other corner, was a workbench and a pin log. A head was drawn on the side and front of it.

The flame danced as she walked down the hallway. Almost kissing the toes of all the marionettes that sat above her on shelves. It sounded like wood splitting as she walked at a quickened pace to answer the door.

She opened the door to a crack, big enough to let her face show and the candlelight. Her eyes were wide in surprise.

Eli was standing there with the box in his arms. His hands were bandaged to the fingertips. The bandages did not stop there. It traveled up his arm and covered his neck and head. Only his eyes and mouth were showing. The right arm was in a sling.

Omi hadn't seen so much hatred in one's eyes.

The wounded boy opened the box and poured the ash, wood splinters, and Shavings' head all over Omi's front porch.

"No thanks!" said Eli. He said it firm and convincingly.

Dragon Fever

Savannah hit the snooze button on her alarm clock for the fifth time. Five extra minutes felt like winning the lottery. However, she did not want to get up. If she got up, she would have to go and take care of her father who wet the bed every morning. There has never been a day that Savannah woke up and found him lying in dry sheets.

At first, taking care of her sickly father—who is sixty-four years of age—felt honorable. After the first week, it began to feel like a chore. By the second month, Savannah was exhausted from all the sleepless nights and the smell of urine-stained sheets. She did not know what was worse, cleaning up after an accident in his pants or cooking the same meals over and over again. Her life was staring to turn into Ground Hogs' Day.

There was no time for herself. She was a slave to her father's needs. How could she be so stupid as to even consider taking care of him? All this work, just so she can get into Heaven?

When was the last time she went out with her girlfriends?

The alarm clock went off again and this time, Savannah rolled her body out of the jaws of her comfortable bed. She did it so fast, because she was afraid, her bed would swallow her up and keep her there the whole morning.

*****

Her father, Ted, sat at the kitchen table like he was frozen in time. His sickness was a rare one—only three cases of it in the past six years.

It started off as fatigue. Occasionally, Ted would stare off into outer space and forget where he was. His hands were shaky, and he began to go blind. His eyes were beginning to turn crimson red, making him look like his eyes were filled with infection.

After a year, his eyes looked like two rubies. Savannah's mother had run off with another man as soon as she found out the news of Ted's health was declining. It broke his heart into a million pieces when she left.

Savannah remembered the day he came home and found her mother leaving in a car with the top down. The man had a beard and his arm wrapped around her shoulders. They both laughed as the car drove away from the house.

Sometimes, Savannah did not know how she was still living with the sort of pain she felt that day. There was barely any money and she watched as her father died slowly and painfully. There were no words to describe how Ted felt.

His tears came out red.

When she thought about this—which was often—it helped her to keep going. Humans are built for struggle and Savannah was tough.

"I made waffles instead of pancakes," said Savannah. "I thought it would be a nice change from the same old pancakes." She put a plate in front of Ted and placed his fork in his hand. "You need to try and fork the food yourself. The doctor said it'll make you stronger."

His eyes looked awful, thought Savannah.

She took a seat next to him and began to eat her breakfast. Savannah tried not to look at her father's death stare while she ate her scrambled eggs. A glob of syrup drizzled down her mouth and it reminded her of the goop that was coming out of his eyes.

In a raspy voice, Ted began to speak. Unexpectedly, Savannah screamed, and she spat out her food.

"I inherited a land," he said, "when I die it will be yours. It was my grandfather's land. But I warn you my daughter of the events that happened there and pray you never go there. Will you hear me?"

*****

Savannah let her father speak. She was awestruck by his words, because he hadn't spoken in such a long time.

"There's gold in that land. It was found by two kids making sandcastles, playing, and running. One of them tripped and fell over something protruding out of the ground."

"It was the size of a soccer ball when they dug it out completely. One of them took their bucket to the lake to get water. They did this so they could soften the dirt and help them pull it out of the hole faster. The child that tripped over it, had hurt himself badly. But he was distracted by the gold they pulled from the earth.”

“Their father told them bedtime stories of pirates and gold. It was all make believe, but not today. The kids had no time to investigate the gold further, because their mothers had arrived and asked them what they found.”

“The two mothers stared in wonder at the gold. They could sell this and they would be able to come out of poverty, almost instantly. What a blessing this was, and it was her child that found it, he had the markings on his leg from tripping over it.”

“Before she could make a move or utter a word, the other mother’s hands reached to the golden ball and ripped it from the child’s grasp. It was the gold that was making them act this way. The mothers were taken over by Dragon Fever. Greed so strong, that it brainwashed their minds and was destroying it.”

“The child that tripped over the gold in the first place, began to cry and crawl toward the mother that had the ball in her arms. She kicked at all three of them. One of her kicks connected with the side of the child’s right temple and killed him instantly.”

“The mothers strangled each other to death and the ball was dropped on the living child’s head. It was horrible. For three days, their bodies and blood stained the ground, until my grandfather sent out a search party to find them. The whole town looked for those families and it was the fathers that lead the search party. Together they found them. The fathers were not ready to see. Their hands turned into fists and they brought them up to their chests and they cried. All the hype, and all the rumors, and all the worry, were true.”

"It didn't take long for them to see the ball of gold laying on top of one of the kid's body. Somebody grabbed it and lifted it up and began to run away with it. He was stopped and pushed backwards, causing him to drop it, then it would be picked up by somebody new. Then they rake off running with it."

"A fist stopped him, and he dropped the ball on top of somebody's toe. A domino effect began within the search party. Every ten minutes, somebody would die. They were beaten to death or died of their injuries from being stomped on."

"By some miracle, one of the search party members lifted his fist and before he delivered it to his neighbor, he looked over to his left, beyond the fighting, and saw a shadow figure that hovered and wielded a weapon."

*****

"I warn you not to go there ever!" he shouted. His eyes began seeping blood and puss.

Savannah lost her appetite and began to cry, silently. She did not know why she was crying. Perhaps it was because she thought her dad's broken heart and that he will die alone.

"I love you, Dad."

*****

Ted died two weeks after he told that story. Was it true? Did he really own a land with buried gold? She could not believe it.

If she was not thinking about her father, she was thinking about the gold. When they buried Ted, Savannah's mom did not show up for the funeral. She did not have to love her dad, but she could have come to show her respects.

A lawyer approached Savannah and explained to her that her father did indeed have a will. There was a list of things he left for her, but it was the Bill-of-Sale for the piece of land that caught Savannah's eye. Her father *was* telling her the truth after all.

It was not until Savannah was having money troubles, that she was entertaining the idea of going down to that piece of land and digging up some of the gold for herself. If she did not pay the bill in a week, she was going to lose her father's house. It would break her heart if that happened. So, she grabbed a shovel and bucket and tossed them into her car.

*****

No Trespassing

The sign was metal and hot to the touch.

Savannah placed her hand on the handle of the gate and quickly pulled it away. It felt like she was burned with fire. She had to rummage through her trunk, so she could find an old shirt that could be used as an oven mitten.

She rested her shovel on her shoulder and let her bucket dangle from her left hand. When she placed her hand on the handle this time, she could feel a warm sensation in her hand with the oven mitten she made.

A screech sound echoed around her. It scared her and the crows that were nearby. They squawked and you could hear them scurry away in fear into the air. There was a breeze that blew past Savannah. It was hot and full of dirt and she had to close her eyes to avoid the dirt from getting in them.

She opened her eyes and walked through the gate. It felt like a desert. It baffled her to see to see the inherited land for herself. There were tumble weeds and dead trees, but mostly there was hot sand. However, that was not what caught her eye.

It was the lake.

*****

Her father's story bounced around in Savannah's mind. He was sick and probably did not know what he was saying. So far, he was telling the truth. Was that why she was scared?

What would she have to be afraid of? Scared of success? Or was it the deaths in her father's story that kept her from being calm? All she had to do was go to the lake and scoop up some water. The water was going to be used to make the sand easier to dig up.

She pushed the shovel into the sand, so she could carry the water with ease. When Savannah looked at the water, she could see straight to the bottom. It was so clean and so blue. It made her smile and feel satisfied. She made a cup with her hand and brought it up to her mouth to drink. It took everything for her to stop drinking and get to work on digging.

When she made it back to her shovel, Savannah poured the bucket out on the ground and watched as the sand drank it up. The Earth was so dry, that it took more than four buckets of water to soften the dirt.

Beads of sweat found their way into Savannah's eyes and it burned them. She took the shirt and tied it around her head like a bandanna. She was determined to find something. Determined to find anything. Determined to find gold.

*****

A few hours went by and Savannah was beginning to make progress with the hole she was digging. She was deep enough that the sand did not swallow up the water right away and she didn't have to make multiple trips to the lake. She wished she dug closer, but according to the story, it was farther out.

The sun was doing a good job at making everything hot and miserable. Savannah took off her shirt, revealing her sweat soaked tank top. Her shoulders were starting to burn and her head began to hurt. If she continued to drink the water, she would have to go to the bathroom and there was not a place for her to go. The car was far away and if she went back to the car, she was going to leave and possibly not come back.

But then she would lose the house. Savannah had to keep going.

She kept digging and digging.

If she didn't get the gold found, she felt like she was going to die from stroke and exhaustion. Right when she was about to give up, her shovel hit something hard and shiny.

There were no words for how she felt when she saw the gold shining in the sun. She poured the rest of the bucket into the hole and the water uncovered the top of a golden ball. Savannah could not believe her eyes. It was going to be worth thousands of dollars and this is just one piece of it.

Savannah dug around it and a few times she thought it was easy enough to break free from the ground, but she found that she needed to dig more. She was hot and tired, but when the golden ball came loose, she felt a surge of energy and was able to lift it over her head and push it out onto the surface.

The sudden jolt of energy and the sudden strength was a result of Dragon Fever. She thought only of the gold and that it was hers. All of it was hers. The land from which the gold came from was her own.

There had to be more. If there is more gold, it was hers too.

She picked up the golden ball and held it to her chest like a baby. It was the size of a basketball. It was beautiful. Savannah could not tell if it was her sweat or her tears that were dripping on the surface of the ball. She began to walk back toward the car and did not notice that she was taking a different route.

The dirt she was shoveling out of the hole, made a small hill to the right and was in the way of her old path. She walked a few feet off to the left, and was too preoccupied with her thoughts.

SNAP!

*****

Savannah did not scream right away, because of the quickness of the bite. It froze her leg in time. Landing on top of the gold and knocking all the air out of her lungs. Never in her whole life, had she felt such pain. Her leg felt like a broken branch, hanging by splinters.

She tried to reach for her stomach and her leg at the same time. Her mouth was gasping for air and she looked like a mime would if they were crying. It took a long time for her catch her breath. When she looked at her legs, she could see that her leg was trapped inside the teeth of a bear trap.

How come there is a bear trap out here? That was the million-dollar question.

There was no doubt that there was metal on bone. It did not break the bone, but it sliced right through her calf. She slowly got to a sitting position and examined the damage. It looked like her limb was in a car wreck. When her fingers touched the metal, she instantly regretted it.

Those horror movies where they try to pry open the teeth came to mind; she was afraid of failing to open it and making it worse.

What was she going to do? Savannah cursed herself for being so stupid. Stepping into a bear trap out in the middle of nowhere was an accident, but she could not help it to think that she made a mistake coming out here without telling anyone.

It was not long before she realized she wasn't alone. It was starting to get cold. Comfortable at first, then it was making her teeth chatter. Savannah's jaw was beginning to feel like a rusty hinge. The blood looked like paint that was chipping away from wear and tear.

That is when Savannah looked at the lake and saw a black hood pop out of the ice.

*****

Her father's voice could be heard inside her head, *"A shadow that hovered and wielding a weapon."*

The shadow was Death and the weapon it wielded is a scythe. It was faceless and had no flesh on its hands. Death floated toward Savannah without a sound.

Savannah knew if she did not get out of the trap, she was going to die. Losing her leg was better than losing her life. She was going to have to shut the trap completely and surrender her leg, so she could get away.

She took the bandanna from her head and wrapped it around her leg; above the trap. It was hard to pull the knot tight with how cold her fingers were. Death had a hand reached out at her but before it could grab her hair, she slammed her fists down on the trap and snapped her leg off.

It felt so good to be free from the trap that Savannah was more relieved than she was in pain. Just a little bit. She could feel the cold on her back as she crawled toward the car. Blood trailed behind her, but it froze as Death gained on her.

Her freedom was cut short when she saw the golden ball blocking her path. Savannah tried to move it, but it was heavy. She rolled on her back in defeat and came face-to-face with the bony finger of Death.

There was nothing more she could do. Savannah closed her eyes and waited to die. She would be with her father soon. Only this time, he would not be sick. He would not have those disgusting red eyes anymore. He would not be giving away scary stories for free.

Nothing happened.

When Savannah opened her eyes, she saw Death holding the ball of gold in its clutch. Death floated over the hole and tossed it back in. The hood looked back over at her and Death pointed at Savannah in warning. It was a matter of seconds before Death turned transparent and disappeared.

The hot sun and its extreme heat returned, and Savannah lay there without a leg. She stared up at the sun and did not close her eyes.

All she could see now was the sun. Savannah closed them and turned her head. When she opened them back up, she came face-to-face with a child's skull.

www.ingramcontent.com/pod-product-compliance
Lightning Source LLC
Chambersburg PA
CBHW071452030726
47593CB00003B/976